9.25.16

Julians

New  ... ... capy.

Don't Share with Sean.

M.

Out of the Storm

Out of the Storm

A Novella

M. Saverio Clemente

RESOURCE *Publications* · Eugene, Oregon

Resource Publications
An Imprint of Wipf and Stock Publishers
199 W. 8th Ave., Suite 3
Eugene, OR 97401

www.wipfandstock.com

PAPERBACK ISBN: 978-1-5326-0244-3
HARDCOVER ISBN: 978-1-5326-0246-7
EBOOK ISBN: 978-1-5326-0245-0

Manufactured in the U.S.A.   JULY 27, 2016

For Tracy

Then out of the storm the Lord spoke . . .

Job 38:1

Acknowledgements

I RECENTLY HAD THE good fortune of stumbling upon a piece of writing I completed in middle school. I was no more than eleven or twelve when I wrote it and my boyishness showed. But when reading through for the first time in nearly two decades, I was struck by one insight that my younger-self had to offer. On the very first page, inscribed in bold, black ink, was the following: "I dedicate this book to all my family and friends who have made my life worth writing about. Thank you to everyone."

Whether or not the life and musings of my grammar-school-self were actually "worth writing about" is tenuous. But the further point—the fact that my writing was and is deeply indebted to every person who has been written into the story of my life—is beyond dispute. I would not be the writer that I am without the people who have made me the man that I am. And so it is only right to acknowledge that this work—like all I write and all I do— has been born out of my relationships with the countless people who, through interactions big and small, have shaped me, made me, brought me to myself.

Thank you to everyone.

Part 1

"Just young," Kitty replied. "Don't worry—I'll break him of the habit."

"He's kind of cute," said Mary. "In an ugly sort of way."

"We're all ugly," Kitty replied. "Some of us just hide it better than others."

"You do a good job hiding it," said Mary. "I'd give anything to look like you."

"No," said Kitty. "Not like me."

"Yes," Mary protested. "If I could look like anyone I'd look just like you."

"Not like me," said Kitty.

For a moment both were silent.

"He is a brute," Kitty started again. She looked over at the hulking twenty-something who stood at the far side of the room with his hands in his pockets and a dumb look on his face. "But that's ok. I only do it for the money."

"Oh, does he have a lot?" asked Mary.

The two laughed.

"Maybe we can do dinner and drinks—like last weekend," said Kitty.

"Only this time, I get the cute one and *you* get stuck with his friend," said Mary.

"We'll see where the night takes us," said Kitty.

"It's a date!" Mary giggled and she kissed Kitty's porcelain white cheek.

"A date," Kitty replied, wiping the ruby lipstick from her face.

Chapter 2

THOMAS HAD HIS DOUBTS. Still, he knew there was something there. Something more. So every Saturday afternoon he drove over to Our Lady of Sorrows and smoked a box of Camel unfiltereds in the parking-lot. It was a small, wooden church two towns over. Unlike his home parish of St. Anthony's—a daunting Cathedral of stone and stained glass—this quaint chapel was no larger than a cabin. The work of poor Irish immigrants, it sat a meager forty parishioners. Yet every Saturday, the Vigil Mass saw its pews filled to the last. A few chivalrous men—having given up their seats to the women who arrived late—even stood at the back of the church. Thomas remained in the front seat of his Chevy, smoking cigarette after cigarette, and watching family after family enter the cramped, oaken parish.

"You think God hears you from out here?" a group of boys had once taunted as they walked down to the field behind the church.

"He forgot about you years ago old man," they jeered.

At least I'm here, thought Thomas and he rolled up his window.

After that, he began parking in the back corner of the lot—away from the field, unseen by the other parishioners.

The tolling of bells signaled the end of Mass. A few eager churchgoers scurried out before the final blessing. Seeing this, Thomas flicked his last cigarette out the window, started the truck, turned on the radio, and pulled out onto the gravel road. The radio cracked and hissed as he scanned through the stations. He settled on a local weather report. They were predicting snow. A lot of snow. Thomas hadn't seen snow since moving to the Valley in the mid-nineties. But now they were predicting snow and it seemed like the only thing anyone was interested in talking about. He had been hearing about it all week. Apparently it would start with light flurries around eight and by morning the roads would be covered.

"There'll be no traffic this weekend," said the weatherman with a laugh. "Residents are being advised to take their cars off the road. Don't plan on going anywhere. Settle in by the space heater and prepare to be there until late Sunday night."

That the snow wasn't supposed to pick up until the early hours of Sunday morning came as welcome news. After keeping vigil outside of the Vigil Mass, Thomas typically took dinner at a local pub. Then he would walk over to a nearby hotel and drown the rest of his evening in middle-shelf scotch. Tonight promised to be no different. He savored the sameness.

Chapter 3

ON THE OTHER SIDE of town, Kitty and Mary were getting dolled up to go out. Saturday night was girls' night. At least it had been for the past few weeks. Girls' night, however, was oddly similar to most nights. Perhaps it gave cause to indulge in an extra mixed drink. But to an outside observer the difference was nearly imperceptible. The two friends went clubbing five or six times a week. Some nights they danced until dawn. Most nights, each found a man to take her home. The next morning, they would meet at a local diner to share stories and laughs.

The stories, they began to notice, had an odd sort of consistency to them. Gentleman X—who was not much of a gentleman—had bought her drink after drink and paid her compliment after compliment. Then, when she was sufficiently drunk, he hailed a cab and they left for her place. There, he admitted to having recognized her. He had seen her do it on screen. He had fantasized about her a hundred times. A thousand. And now, to have her here: in the flesh. It was almost more than he could bear. He knew—he knew!—that he would be the best lover she'd ever known. He was wild and passionate—grabbing her, pushing her against the wall, kissing her with all of his might. He tore off his clothes. Then hers. He grunted and growled and sang. He was lost and free. Wild and lost and free.

Then something happened. He began to think. His mind raced. Reason replaced instinct. He realized that he had no business being with a woman like this. He could never live up to the others. The others! How many others? How many had come before? All of them more experienced. All of them more knowledgeable. All more physically gifted. How could he compare? He couldn't. Only a fool would think he could. He was making a fool of himself. At this very moment. He was making a fool of himself right now. Was she enjoying this? Was he? Was anyone even enjoying this? What if he touched her here? What if he kissed her there? No. No, she wasn't enjoying it. Not at all. And neither was he.

Wait. Wait, what was that noise? That noise she just made? Was she moaning? Was she sighing? Was she laughing? She was laughing. She was laughing! She was laughing at him! Wait. She let out a moan. Yes, she let out a slight moan. He was sure of it. He heard it. But what was it? Was it pleasure? Was it passion? No. No, it was laughter. It was laughter at him! She was laughing at him. At this moment. Laughing. How could he compare? He couldn't. How would he please her? He wouldn't. What was he thinking? What was he doing? How should he act? What should he say? Who should he be?

No, he was doomed. Yes, doomed. He was doomed from the start. And in a matter of moments, he went from wild and lost and free to mechanical and awkward and doomed. He had lost himself in passion and found himself in shame. Try as he might, he fell flat. There was nothing to be done. He knew it was over. He had fallen.

"Don't fret," she told him sweetly. "It wasn't your fault. You were doomed from the start."

After getting dressed, she walked him to the door and, with a final patronizing kiss, sent him on his way.

This was how the story went. This was how each story went. Morning after morning, coffee after coffee, recap after recap. They were all the same. They were all always the same. The circumstances varied from time to time—what he said or how he said it. But in the end, they were all the same. All always the same. And after a while, these once entertaining failures lost their charm. They used to be the source of endless laughter. But the repetition had become so repetitive. It had become monotonous. It was a bore. So in order to break up the sameness, the girls devised a new approach. They decided to make a game of it. And they played for keeps.

Chapter 4

THE RAGGED URCHIN WASN'T Thomas's favorite pub. It wasn't anyone's. But it was cheap and it was quiet and it was dark. It had food and beer and scotch and tables. It had places to sit and places to piss and it had a middle-aged mother of four with a fat belly and a prosthetic leg to bring you your food and tell you when you were drunk. If you didn't stare at her leg, she talked to you sweetly. If you asked about her four children, she gave you an extra pickle with your burger. She didn't expect a tip and always seemed surprised and grateful when she got one. She was pleasant enough and only spoke to customers who spoke to her.

She spoke affectionately of her late husband—how he was a tireless worker and a loving father. It was the work, she often said, that killed him. He'd wanted to be able to send their four children to school. He'd wanted to provide. He worked for them. He died for them. And when he stopped by each week to leave them with her at the end of her Sunday night shift—the court had seen fit to give him custody on weekends—no one asked any questions. To her he was dead. And so he was.

The Ragged Urchin wasn't Thomas's favorite pub but it was the pub at which he took his Saturday night dinners. He'd been doing so for almost a year. Before that, he was a regular at another bar which he liked much better. He'd been a regular there for almost a decade. Then the owner fell ill. When his son took over the business, he instituted a number of changes. The dark, dank, quiet, bar where Thomas was accustomed to eating dinner without being bothered became a trendy night club full of twenty-somethings just out of college.

For the first few months, Thomas attempted to ignore the changes. He was the type of man who would rather adapt than go through the hassle of finding a new place. And to some extent, he was successful. The one good thing about humans, he often reminded himself, is that they can get used to anything. Then he would look around his new habitat and remember that it is also the worst thing about humans.

He was forced to find The Ragged Urchin after a slight altercation at his old pub. It was shortly after happy hour one Saturday night and the young crowd was starting to file in. Thomas had just finished eating. He stared at the white head of his beer which tossed and turned along the bottom of his glass like the frothy foam which crashed along the coast the morning after a storm. As he considered whether or not to order another drink, something on the other side of the bar caught his attention. One of the young patrons—just a boy, really—was barking out orders at the frightened girl seated next to him. She had a sweet face and long, brown hair and she looked as if she was about to cry. It was clear by their body language that she and he had entered together and that—as young girls often do—she'd done something to make him jealous. Asserting himself, the boy grabbed her by the arm and began to insist, forcefully, that they leave.

Thomas scanned the bar and noticed that, of the few patrons who had looked up from their phones, no one was willing to intervene. He wiped the corners of his mouth with his napkin and got up from the table. He crossed the bar with a few quick strides and, when he reached the frantic couple, dug his fingers into the pressure point located between the boy's shoulder and his neck. The boy cringed and released the girl instantly. He stood—frozen in place.

"Sir," said Thomas. "I would appreciate it if you would leave this nice young lady alone."

He smiled kindly at the girl and noticed that her eyes, red and full of tears, seemed to whisper an unheard *thank you*.

Then her fist struck Thomas square in the groan. As he doubled over in pain, he looked up at her innocent face. It was red and full of tears.

"Fuck you, old man," she said. "Mind you own goddamned business."

"Fuck you, old man," said the boy and he buried his fist in Thomas's back.

Thomas fell to the floor. He felt the boy's boot thump against his ribs. He heard a loud crack. Then he felt nothing. He touched his hand to the back of his head. It was wet. He wasn't sure if it was blood or perspiration or if they had spit on him. He lay there—beaten and broken.

When the commotion settled and all was said and done, the manager attended to the defeated old man.

"I'm going to have to ask you to leave," he said in an unsympathetic voice.

"Makes sense," said Thomas.

"And don't come back, you do-goody old fuck," said the manager as Thomas walked out.

"I could've done without that," Thomas said.

But manager had already closed the door behind him.

Chapter 5

"ONE OF THE MORE interesting things about this industry is that every performer has her own name and her own reason for choosing it . . ."

"That's one of the more interesting things about this industry?" said Kitty with a smile.

"Fair," laughed the interviewer. "Regardless, each name has a special meaning. Tell our readers the significance of yours."

"Well," said Kitty. "I remember my grandma—she raised my brother and me when my mom was real sick. She always used to pray to St. Clare. She wore a St. Clare medal and had a St. Clare statue in her bedroom and when she died, St. Clare was on the Mass card. She was an important person in my grandma's life and my grandma was an important person in mine. It just seemed to work."

"And Kitty?" asked the man intently.

"Kitty . . ." she paused. "Now that's a different story."

"Different stories sell magazines," said the man.

"My pictures sell magazines," Kitty corrected.

"Fair," said the man. "But Kitty," he tried again. "Why Kitty?"

Had she been honest, she would have told him the ability to choose a new name really was one of the more appealing parts of working in the business. When she was born, she was given a name. She hadn't had a say. Who asked her? Who said, *is this who you want to be?* Who said, *are you ok with this?* No one. No one gave a shit. No one cared that this wasn't who she wanted to be.

No one cared that she wasn't ok with it. If anyone had bothered to ask, she would have said no from the start. She would have stopped before she even began. But no one asked. No one cared. And here she was.

Then she entered the business. When she agreed to do it on screen, she was given a new name. Better: she chose a new name. Kitty St. Clare. She was Kitty St. Clare. No one asked. She chose. She took St. Clare for her grandmother—the woman who raised her. The only one who loved her. And Kitty—she took Kitty for Kitty. The only one she loved.

Kitty was the neighborhood cat. She was a stray with black fur and a white belly. She had double paws and white whiskers and a small tumor that hung from her hind thigh and made her limp on the right side. She had matted fur and oval eyes and when she purred, her whole body shook. She never meowed and she never hissed and sometimes she would bring you a dead mouse or baby rabbit to prove that she was worth loving. She rubbed up against the legs of strangers and she let the neighborhood kids pick her up and carry her for blocks or put her in the baskets on fronts of their bikes and ride even further. She liked milk and she liked being pet and if you were having a bad day she would lick your boot until you laughed and felt better. She was a good cat and she went by the name Kitty and the neighborhood kids adored her.

One day—back before Kitty who does it on screen did it on screen, back before she'd taken the name Kitty in honor of her childhood pet—Kitty the neighborhood cat came looking for attention. It was just after Kitty who does it on screen's mom got sick and just before Kitty who does it on screen's grandma moved in and taught the children how to pray to St. Clare. It was then that Kitty the neighborhood cat came looking for attention. She purred and purred as Kitty who does it on screen rubbed her soft underbelly.

"Why you messing with that stupid cat?" asked Kitty's older brother. "Ma said not to play with it."

"She's not hurting anyone," said Kitty who does it on screen—just a girl.

"Ma said not to play with it. She said it's a flea bag. She said it's been making her sick."

"Mom didn't say that!" Kitty protested.

"She did too."

"Did not."

"Did too, did too, did too! She said it's been giving her headaches and stomachaches and backaches. She said it's the reason dad left and she can't find a decent man and she's all alone. She said it's why her life's shit."

"No she didn't."

"She said she regrets the day it was born and that she'd like to hold its head in the bathtub until it can't breathe no more just to watch it suffer like she suffers."

"Stop! Stop it!"

"She said if she could she'd crush its ugly little face."

"Stop!" Kitty shouted. "Leave us alone. We're just playing."

"Playing?" said her brother. "Playing?"

"Playing," repeated the girl.

Her brother's boot struck the unsuspecting cat and sent it flying.

"Playing!" he screamed as he chased it down the dead end street. "Playing! Playing!"

"Stop!" his sister cried.

He cornered the cat and booted it again.

It scurried off and hid in a nearby gutter.

After that, Kitty the cat didn't come around as much. She became skittish and scared and she cried and hissed when the neighborhood kids approached. Worse, she would sit for hours and hours licking the same patch of fur until the fur was gone and all that was left was a swollen red sore where fur and flesh had once been. Then she would lick the sore until it bled and bled. Then she would lick the blood.

"Kitty," said the man once more. "What made you choose the name Kitty?"

There was a long pause.

"Tell me your story," the man broke the silence.

"I wish I had one," Kitty shrugged. "I guess I just thought my fans would find it sexy."

"That's it?" said the man.

"That's it," said Kitty.

"Well, I'm sure our readers will agree. It is sexy. Very sexy."

Chapter 6

THE RAGGED URCHIN WASN'T Thomas's favorite pub. But there he was and there he would be until he finished his dinner and his beer and, if he was in the mood, his second beer. Then he would finish his night across the street in the bar of a nearby hotel where he would drown the rest of his night in middle-shelf scotch. He wouldn't speak unless spoken to and even then he probably wouldn't speak. It promised to be a good night.

"How are the kids, Mindy?" asked the man at the table next to him.

Thomas recognized the man. He too took his Saturday night dinners at The Ragged Urchin. And he always made a point of asking the waitress—the middle-aged mother of four with a fat belly and a prosthetic leg—about her kids. He always had a story of his own and a smile on his face. He was a real prick.

"They grow up so fast," said the one-legged waitress. She let out a reminiscent sigh.

"Faster than last week?" the man said with a smile.

"Faster by the day!" she exclaimed.

Thomas glared at the two of them with resentment. He knew that she'd soon hobble her way back to the kitchen only to emerge a short while later with an extra pickle. Thomas didn't like pickles. But knowing that that prick was going to get an extra one—that rubbed him the wrong way. He stopped listening to their conversation and instead mused on how happy it would make him to break the man's jaw.

Happy enough, he concluded.

Then, as the one-legged waitress limped away, he watched her limp and imagined what it would be like to be with her. Thomas was not attracted to her. Not in the least. Still, he imagined being with her. He imagined her breathing heavy and kissing him softly. He imagined him breathing heavy and kissing her with a passion, an excitement he hadn't felt in years. He imagined just how he would undress her—sliding his right hand up the back of her shirt and undoing her bra, then pulling shirt and bra off with one fluid motion. He imagined how she would undress him—unbuttoning his shirt one button at a time and sliding it over his broad shoulders. He imagined her on her back and him pressing his hard belly—hardened by the years and by the scotch—down upon her. He imagined her chin in his mouth and his hand on her thigh—the good one. He imagined her moaning ever so softly and he imagined himself grunting then laughing at himself for grunting. He imagined the two of them laughing at his grunting and then her kissing his forehead and each one of his eyelids and his nose and his mouth. He imagined rolling off of her and her gesturing for him to come a bit closer. And he imagined lying in her arms and crying softly upon her breasts while she rubbed her stumpy fat fingers through what was left of his thin black hair.

This wasn't the first time that such a scenario had played out in Thomas's mind. And he wasn't alone. Patrons often expressed an interest in the plain waitress. They usually began to notice her sometime between their sixth and seventh beers. Then the talk would begin. The novelty of it. They always spoke of the novelty of it. A woman with one leg. She was so unusual. So exotic. What was she like? What was it like? The novelty. The leg.

But these were not Thomas's interests. It was her meekness. It was her humility. She was nothing like the women he had known in his younger days. She was more like his mother. She was nothing like the women he had known. She was more honest. More herself. She had a fat belly and small breasts, a masculine face and eyes that looked as if they'd shed more tears than any eye should shed. She had a fake leg and she hobbled and limped and her fingers were stumpy and they were fat and the nails on her fingers had been chewed down to their beds. She looked tired and she looked worn and she slouched forward with rounded shoulders and a rounded back which looked tired and worn. She had stains on her shirt and stains on her jeans and she lied about her husband being dead and she looked worn and tired and stained. But she was honest. She was herself.

Thomas had only ever seen one other woman look so honest. He had only ever seen one other woman look herself. And he'd made that woman his wife. But now he sat alone at The Ragged Urchin sipping his beer and watching this woman limp from table to table. As he did, he tried to remember what it was like to make love to someone so humble, so honest, so true, so real.

Chapter 7

THE SEX WAS NEVER pleasurable. It was always uncomfortable. Often it was painful. It wasn't sex, really. It could be called fucking. But even that seemed generous. It was more uncomfortable than anything else. Except for when it was painful. Then it was more painful than anything else. And this time it had been painful.

"You were right," said Kitty. "He was grabby."

"Did it hurt?" asked the young Egyptian.

"It did," she said. "It did."

The two were silent.

"Well, don't just stand there," Kitty said. "Come in and have a drink."

Mary followed Kitty into the cramped apartment. The door squeaked shut behind them.

"Place looks good," said Mary.

"I've been feeling a bit scattered," said Kitty. "Just needed to clean something. When I feel that way, I clean and clean."

"When I feel that way, I drink."

"That too," Kitty smiled.

She lived in a humble studio apartment. She slept on a lofted bed under which sat a torn futon and a side table with a lamp. The bulb in the lamp had burnt out months ago. She hadn't gotten around to replacing it. The apartment had two large windows which faced the red Valley sun as it set over the buildings across the street. On the windowsill sat a pot with fresh cut lilies as clean and as white as snow. On the fridge was a Christmas card from her nieces and nephews. She had only ever seen them once. Thanksgiving—three years ago. She'd flown home for the weekend and stayed at her brother's place. There, she got drunk on red wine and told the youngest that Santa wasn't real and that the gifts were from her dad and that he gave her more than she deserved because he still felt guilty about forcing his first girlfriend to have an abortion and that that was why they went to church on Sundays and why he made them say "Happy birthday Jesus" on Christmas morning and that none of it mattered much anyway because we'll all be dead soon enough. She wasn't invited back.

Yet she still received a Christmas card each November which she hung on the fridge with a magnet from the Restless Hearts Gentlemen's Club. On the magnet was the black silhouette of a naked woman. The points of her nipples were clearly visible. She wore stilettos. Above her head was the inscription *Thursday Nights: Amateur Night* in electric blue cursive. Below her feet: *The most beautiful women on earth.*

The neighbors in the studio upstairs could be heard shouting and hitting one another. They were drunk and they were shouting and slamming doors and hitting one another and opening doors and slamming them again. He had drank the last of the vodka and it wasn't fair because it wasn't his to drink and she was out of money because he was a deadbeat who never took care of her like he promised her dying mother he would and she was going to leave him and find a new man who could provide for her and he was fine with that because she was nothing but a no good whore who threw herself at every man she met and he had no right to call her a whore but he did it anyway because he had no respect for women and especially not for her and she deserved respect because she worked too and she worked just as hard as he did and he was lazy and he was fat and he was bald now and he looked nothing like he did in high school and he never wanted to fuck like he use to but that was only because he was bored with her and she was fat now too and she didn't care what she looked liked anymore and besides why did he need her if he had the computer and it did the job just fine and who gave a shit anyway because we'll all be dead soon enough.

"Sit," said Kitty and she pointed to the futon.

"On that?" Mary giggled.

"Where else?" asked Kitty.

"It's just," Mary paused. "I've heard stories about what happens on that."

"Oh you've heard stories, have you?"

Mary nodded.

"You're the subject of some of the stories!" Kitty exclaimed.

"True enough," Mary laughed and she sat.

Kitty walked over to the kitchenette and returned with a liter of rum, a bottle of Coke, and two beer glasses.

"No fair!" Mary protested. "You started without me."

The rum was about two-thirds of the way full.

"Well," Kitty said. "You were late."

"I was caught in traffic. You know how bad it can be on Saturday's. Besides, everyone's out buying stuff for the storm."

"Give it up Mary," said Kitty. "I worked today. I needed a drink."

"I worked too," said Mary.

"Working alone isn't the same," said Kitty. "You know that."

"I know," said Mary. "But I'm broke. It's not fair you started without me. I helped pay for that too."

"You're right," said Kitty. "I'm sorry. I haven't felt myself lately. I just needed a drink, that's all."

"It's ok," said Mary halfheartedly. "I get it."

"I'll tell you what," said Kitty. "Why don't I buy you a couple of drinks tonight to make it up to you?"

The two laughed. Neither of them would be buying drinks. That's what men were for.

Chapter 8

BEFORE HEADING OVER TO Our Lady of Sorrows, Thomas had stopped to buy a pack of Camel unfiltereds at a corner store. There had been a line and he had had to wait and he had been annoyed that there was a line and that he had had to wait. Apparently people were out buying supplies for the storm—water and canned goods and toilet paper, beer and wine and smokes. He observed the mild panic and laughed to himself. Where he was from, schools didn't close unless there was over a foot of snow. Where he was from, work didn't close unless there was over two. Where he was from, bars didn't close period. But this wasn't where he was from. This was the Valley. And Thomas hadn't seen snow since moving to the Valley in the mid-nineties. The people here were told to be prepared and so they were out preparing to be prepared. If they just had food in their pantries, batteries in their flashlights, locks on their doors—then they'd be safe.

As he stood waiting to buy his cigarettes and periodically checking his watch, Thomas noticed a boy—no older than ten or twelve—in the back corner of the corner store. He watched as the boy glanced quickly over each shoulder and then stuffed a bag of cool ranch chips into the oversized pouch on the front of his oversized sweatshirt. Thomas looked at the cashier who was reading a text message on his phone and filling an eco-friendly, biodegradable bag with milk and eggs and bread and batteries for the woman at the counter.

"Would you like a copy of your receipt?" he asked.

"Mmm . . . No thanks," said the woman. "My purse has enough junk in it."

She laughed and looked back at Thomas.

Thomas did not laugh.

"Oh, sorry," said the cashier as he tore a slip of paper from the register. "I'm used to just printing them."

"What's one more thing?" she said sweetly.

As she stuffed the receipt into her purse, Thomas saw that it really was full of junk. Then he looked back at the boy who now stood, browsing through the magazine rack, attempting to look as inconspicuous as possible.

"There something I can help you find, son?"

The sudden break in the seemingly endless shuffle of background noise shook the boy and made him jump. When he turned, he found himself standing face to face with a hulking man of about fifty. The man had a dark beard, thick black-framed glasses, and a single, blotted tattoo on his left forearm. There was a square button pinned to his shirt which said *Store Manager, Hunter* in bold black print. Thomas considered the possibility that the word following the comma was not the man's name but a second title.

"Nahh . . . No sir," stuttered the boy.

"Oh no?"

"No sir," repeated the boy.

"Well alright then," grunted the man. "You just let me know if there's something I can help you with."

"Yes, sir. Thank you, sir. I will, sir."

The boy let out a sigh of relief and turned toward the exit.

"Hey boy," the man's voice shattered the shuffle once more.

The boy froze.

"Boy," repeated the man.

"Yes?" The boy slowly turned and faced him.

"Did you forget something?"

The boy's heart sank.

"Your wallet," said the man. He waved a dark piece of brown leather in the air.

"Oh," said the boy. "Thank you, sir."

"Wouldn't want to leave that behind," said the man.

"No sir," said the boy. "Thank you, sir."

He retrieved his wallet and again turned to exit. When he reached the threshold of the door, he paused. Thomas watched as he shrugged, pulled the bag of chips from the pouch on the front of his sweater, placed it on the counter, and quickly scurried out.

"Would you like a copy of your receipt?" the cashier asked the next customer as the register spit out a slip of white paper. His eyes were still glued to his phone.

The manager slowly approached the counter. He picked up the unopened bag of chips, returned it to its place on the shelf, and retreated back into his office.

Chapter 9

THEY WERE DRUNK BEFORE they left for the bar. But if you'd seen them, you would have sworn that they hadn't had a drink all night. If they'd learned one thing from their time in the business it was how to drink. How to be numb. Their coworkers called them actresses. So they knew how to drink and they knew how to act and they knew how to be numb. They knew how to do all three and they knew how to do all three at once and they knew how to do all three well. They drank enough to be drunk and they acted as if they were sober. They drank enough to be numb and they acted as if they felt. But tonight, they hadn't drank enough to be drunk enough to not care if they were drunk or numb or acting or just plain miserable. They needed something to drink. So upon entering the bar, they immediately began their search for a couple of cute guys who could give them what they wanted.

"Buy me a drink," said Mary.

"Do I know you?" asked the man.

"Not yet," said Mary. "But buy me a drink and you'll get to."

"What are you having?" he asked.

"You're buying," she said. "Your choice."

The man signaled to the bartender.

"Buy one for my friend too," she said.

"What is this?" he protested.

"Shut up already," said Mary and she licked the side of his face.

The man leaned in and gave his order across the bar.

"Bud Light?" snapped Mary. "Is that how you treat a lady?"

"First," said the man, "the beers are chasers. Second, the two of you aren't ladies. And third, if you feel slighted now, you're going to be very upset when you see how I treat you later."

Mary slapped him.

Then she kissed him.

Then they all took tequila shots which they chased with the beers.

Then she kissed him some more.

"Can I ask you something?" the man's friend said to Kitty.

"Shoot," said Kitty.

"Are you . . . "

"Am I . . . ?"

"Are you like . . . in movies?"

"I am."

"Like . . . like the kind you find online?"

"Among other places, yes."

"Are you . . . "

"You're going to have to speak up, sweetie. I can't hear you over the sound of the speakers."

"Yeah," he laughed. "It's loud in here."

She sighed.

"So do you like to go out?"

"Why else would I be here, darling?"

"Right. Good point."

Kitty leaned on her hands and watched as her friend pulled the man at the bar in close. He sunk his fangs into her neck and began to suck. She let out a girlish giggle then wrapped her arms around him tight.

Kitty rolled her eyes.

"So . . . so, do you like what you do?" the man's friend interrupted her attempt to avoid him.

"Do I like being fucked?" she asked.

He paused.

"Ugh . . . I guess so. Yeah," he tried.

"No," she said plainly. "I don't."

Kitty grabbed Mary by the arm and pulled her away from her new boy. His teeth marks left a fresh, red imprint on her neck.

"What is it?" asked Mary.

"I have to use the bathroom," said Kitty.

"So use it," said Mary.

"Come with me."

"I'm kind of busy at the moment."

"Come with me," she insisted.

"Fine," Mary said. "Be right back boys."

"We'll be here," said the man at the bar.

His friend ordered another drink and slouched down on a nearby stool.

"What's wrong with you?" asked Mary as they entered the stuffy bathroom.

"This is boring," Kitty protested. "I'm bored."

"Oh don't be a pain," said Mary. "You're just upset that I've found a cute guy to buy me drinks and talk sweet to me."

"He's doing a lot more sucking than talking," she said.

"And what if he is?" said Mary. "What's wrong with that?"

"Come on," said Kitty. "He's an ass."

"Even if he is," said Mary. "I'm having fun."

"Bull," said Kitty. "This place sucks. I'm bored. I'm so bored. I'm always so bored. It's always the same and I'm always bored!"

"What do you want me to do about it?" asked Mary.

"I don't know. Can't we go somewhere? Can't we do something? Can't we be something? Something different? For once?"

"Like what?" asked Mary.

"I thought you wanted to fuck with the locals. Like last weekend. That was fun. That's always fun."

"Always?"

"At least it's different. Let's mix things up a bit. It's a game. It's a challenge."

"It is something different," Mary agreed.

"Then it's settled. We'll ditch this place. We'll ditch these guys. We'll find a local bar full of locals and we'll do something different. Something fun."

"I don't know," said Mary.

"Come on," said Kitty. "It'll be a good night."

"You promise?"

"I promise," said Kitty. "A good night."

Chapter 10

ON THE DAY SHE died, there was a storm out over the Pacific. Dry thunder crashed and cracked and rolled in the grey salt air and black waves broke black and silver on the stony shore. Every so often, a flash of white would tear through the black clouds and the water would glimmer and sparkle and glow. Then it would fade back to an ominous violet which locked the fleeting light beneath its black waves. Thomas stood next to his old Chevy and watched as the waves swallowed the beach. But the beach was resilient. It refused to be ingested. It split the belly of the waves and reemerged once more. The two warred on.

His truck was parked on a steep ridge which overlooked a small town. The town was located on the water's edge. Dozens of sailing vessels lined its docks. An impenetrable fog had settled in over the water. Sea and sky combined to make a single, towering wall of black. The storm was mounting. It crashed and cracked and beat against the shore. And the shore too was black. And the town. Between bursts of thunder, a deadness filled the air. The town was vacant. The last of its residents had packed up their belongings and fled to higher ground. It crouched silently beneath the storm like a Cold War child awaiting nuclear fallout under his desk. It shook with thunder and was silent. It shook and was silent. Its boats had no sailors. Its stables no horses. Its schoolyards no children. Its churches no bells. Then it shook. Then it was silent. It shook and was silent. And all was still.

The crashing waves, the shrieking gulls, the haunting gong of an unseen buoy lost in the deep—these were the only noises that Thomas heard. These were the sounds of what was left. Thomas breathed in the salt air and let the salt and sea sit in his lungs. It stung his lungs and he coughed and spit. Then he lit a cigarette. His first in nearly ten months. He breathed in the tar and tobacco and ash and wished that he could stop thinking and stop feeling and stop breathing and stop wishing. He wished that he could do something. Anything. Then he wished that he could do nothing. Less than nothing. There was nothing to be done. He was as hopeless and as helpless as the tiny town which stood on the water's edge. He was as hopeless as the town which would soon be rocked and ravaged and swallowed and forgotten beneath the waves of the great storm.

The storm, thought Thomas. The storm will be remembered. The destruction. The wreckage. The loss. The storm will be remembered. But what about the town? What about its people? The ones who lose their homes, the ones who lose their jobs, the ones who lose themselves—will they be remembered? Who will remember? Who will tell their stories? Who will keep them after they're gone?

And her. Will she been remembered? Who will remember her? Who will remember how her hair smelled when it was wet with rain? Who will remember how she sneezed every time she chewed mint gum? Who will remember what her fingers felt like when they were wrapped around his or what her eyelashes felt like when they rustled against his cheek or what her smile felt like when she buried her face in his neck? Who will remember how she used to laugh until she cried? Whenever she laughed, she always laughed until she cried. Who will remember how she used to cry until she laughed? Her tears always seemed to end with laughter. Who will remember the time she spilled an entire bowl of spaghetti on his new boss at the company picnic? Who will remember when he taught her how to drive stick and she crashed into the neighbor's mailbox but refused to stop—how she dragged it under the car for blocks? Who will remember their first date? Their first kiss? Their last? Who will remember how she took his hand in hers and pressed it to her face—how her tears ran over his knuckles and how he kissed her forehead and told her not to worry, that he'd be back in the morning? Who will remember how he stopped in the doorway and watched to make sure she was asleep before he left? Who will remember how he stayed even when he knew she was asleep—just to watch? Who will remember how he was awoken by a phone call—how he'd raced to the hospital? Who will remember the doctor's face or the nurse's tears or the slow, melodic breaths which slowed and slowed and slowed? Who will remember his fist through the wall and the hole in the wall and the blood on his knuckles? Who will remember their weekend in Cancun and their day trips to the shore and the nights they sat together reading the same book at the same pace, pausing every few chapters to make love and talk about the how academics aren't content with ruining poetry—now they're trying to ruin prose too?

Who will remember?

I will, he thought. I'll remember. I'll remember it all. Every minute of it. If I remember nothing else, I'll remember it all.

Then he coughed and hacked and coughed and coughed.

"And when you're gone," he said to himself. "Who will remember then?"

He dropped his cigarette to the ground, put it out with his foot, got into his truck, and drove away.

Chapter 11

THEY NEVER TOLD HER how her mother died. They told her that she was sick and that she had to go away. They told her that her grandmother would be taking care of her and her brother until she was well. They told her that the doctors were helping and that the medicine was helping and that her mother was getting better— each day she was getting better. They told her that she'd be home soon and that life would go back to normal. They told her that her mother loved her and that she'd be home soon and that life would go back to normal. Then they told her that they were taking her to Sears. It was time to buy a new dress. Her mother was dead and she needed to look presentable at the funeral.

They never told her how her mother died and she didn't care. She was mad at her mother. Mad at her for getting sick. Mad at her for going away. Mad at her for dying. Her mother was selfish, she decided. She was selfish and, more than that, she was a bad mother. She had never cared about her. She had never cared about her own daughter. If she had, she wouldn't have left. If she had, she wouldn't have died. She'd still be here.

Someday, years from now, when Kitty is old and wrinkled and she has a woman to mash up her carrots and feed them to her on a spoon and to lower the blinds and get her in and out of bed and to wash her off when she's soiled herself and when she has a room-mate whom she doesn't know and when she can still think but has no energy to say what she's thinking and when people assume she's lost her mind because she won't say what she's thinking and when all she does all day long is ignore the TV and think of the past—on that day, she'll remember how many nights she spent unable to sleep, staring at the ceiling, wishing her mother was still alive so that she could die all over again. Then she'll realize what she never wanted to realize. Then she'll know what she never wanted to know. She'll know how her mother died and why she died and how much pain she must have been in and she'll remember the tears and the booze and the struggle and the sorrow and the pain. She'll wonder if it hurts to die and she'll wonder if dying hurts more than living and she'll wonder if Jesus came for her mother and if Jesus and her mother are still waiting for her or if they've forgotten about her after all these years. Then the tears will flow. They'll run from her old, grey eyes and they'll pour down her old, grey cheeks and they'll stain her old, withered face. She'll cry and cry and cry until the woman who feeds her comes to check her vitals and then she'll cry some more. The woman will close the blinds and check if she's soiled herself and fluff her pillow and ask her what's wrong. She'll be too tired to answer and the woman will call the nurse and the nurse will call the doctor and the doctor will diagnose her with pain and suffering and misery and neuropathy. She'll hear them talk about how they're going to drug her and she'll hear her health care proxy say that he doesn't care what they do so long as they get her to stop crying and she'll feel the needle pierce her flesh and it'll miss the vein and the nurse will cuss and it'll pierce her flesh again and she'll cry and cry and cry. Then she'll fall asleep.

Someday, years from now, Kitty will find her peace. Someday, she'll cry until she finds her peace. And then she'll cry some more.

Chapter 12

Sometimes when he crossed the street, he'd take a deep breath, close his eyes, and not open them again until he had safely reached the other side. This was not one of those times. This time, he was in the mood for a glass of scotch—or three. This time, he had to make it across the street in order to get that scotch.

When he stepped out of the musty bar into the brisk winter night, a gust of icy wind cracked and splintered over his red face and he shivered and shook. It was a brisk night and it was winter and it was icy and it was snowing. The snow fell white and it fell hard and the wind blew gusts and circles which spun and danced and the snow fell hard and white. For a minute, Thomas thought of Christmas and of eggnog and of midnight Mass when the dim church is lit only by the dim light of wax candles—how the flames cast oblong shadows on the stone walls and how they flicker and dance. He thought of laughter and of games and of carols and pies and cakes and stuffing and turkey. He thought of the last embers of a warm Christmas fire—watching them dwindle to ash and ember and dust. He thought of home.

"Get the fuck out of the street, old man!" shouted the cabbie and he laid on his horn.

Thomas jumped back to the curb. There he was confronted by the mocking laughter of a group of teens who were out for an evening walk in the snow. But they soon lost interest in him. One of them scooped up a handful of slush from the pavement, formed it into a ball, and threw it at the others. They sprinted off—laughing and kicking and screaming all the way.

"Assholes," Thomas muttered to no one. Then he continued across the street.

Once inside the hotel bar, he found a table in the corner and signaled the waiter. The man hurried over with a glass of scotch on the rocks.

"And how are you this evening, sir?"

"Wet," he said.

"So it's started to come down out there?"

Thomas's grunt was answer enough.

The man nodded and turned to walk away.

"Make sure you keep 'em coming," Thomas called after him.

"I will, sir," said the waiter over his shoulder.

Thomas inhaled the sweet, smoky aroma of the scotch. He let his first sip sit at the back of his throat until it burned the back of his throat. Then he swallowed. It went down hard. The first sip always did. But each time he raised the glass to his mouth, it got a bit easier. Each time, it burned a bit less. And before long, he was thoroughly enjoying it.

As he savored his first glass, he was content to focus on the scotch alone. He gently tilted the tumbler from side to side and watched as the liquor shifted and tumbled and rolled. It ran like molasses down the walls of the glass and then plunged back into the depths. He smelt it. He sipped it. He savored it. He let it burn.

But after his second glass and his third and his fourth, he lost interest in the drink. He drew back and retreated further into himself. He was no longer content. He had become an observer—removed from the room, watching from afar. He studied his fellow patrons as an anthropologist might study some exotic tribe. He studied himself as a scientist might study a corpse—prodding and probing and dissecting. He laid down his judgments and his judgments were harsh and no one heard them but him and he alone was the judge of his judgments. Yet he was the tribesman, the patient, the corpse.

Then she entered. He observed her immediately. He watched as she brushed the snow out of her hair and off her shoulders and as she threw her short, black jacket over the short, wooden stool by the bar. He watched as she adjusted her bra and straightened her skirt and rubbed her arms, warming them from the cold. He watched as she found a seat and ordered a drink and pouted her lips which looked pouty and soft and ready to be kissed. He watched as she slowly sipped her drink and ran her fingers through her hair and laughed and giggled and curled her hair in her fingers. Then he watched some more.

She had a way about her. A sort of confidence. The kind of confidence that most people envy. The kind of confidence that takes years to develop. The kind of confidence that hides pain. She was cute and she was young and she had a sweet face and soft dimples and sincere eyes. But her face was coated with makeup and her eyes were hidden behind eyeliner and her shirt was cut too low and her skirt was cut too high and her boots made her too tall and the men who were looking at her weren't interested in her sweet face or her soft dimples or her honest eyes and neither was Thomas. He watched as she scanned the bar and he wondered what a girl like her was doing in a place like this. It's not that it was a bad hotel. It just wasn't her scene. Girls like her don't spend their Saturday nights at local bars where locals go for a casual drink. Girls like her have men by the handful and drinks by the dozen and they live fast and they party hard and they go to clubs and they dance and laugh and fuck and sing. Girls like her are on TV or in the movies or on the covers of magazines. Girls like her know how to have fun.

Her friend was there too but Thomas didn't care. If the first hid her beauty behind makeup, the second's beauty came from makeup and Thomas had always preferred a natural beauty to an artificial one. Some men like it when a girl gets dolled up. Thomas wasn't one of those men. He wanted a woman who felt comfortable—no blush, no mascara, no foundation. Naked. It was more honest that way. It was more real.

By now, the scotch had gone to his head and he had lost himself in himself and in his observations and in his thoughts and in the scotch. And he was losing himself in her. He forgot that he was old enough to be her father or, God forbid, her grandfather and he forgot that he forgot. Instead, he sat and drank and thought and watched. He watched as guy after guy approached her table and as one by one she sent them away. He watched as her and her friend giggled and taunted and teased the men into offering them drinks and he watched as they declined the offers. He watched her laugh. He watched her smile. He watched her flirt. He watched her seduce. And then he watched some more.

She knows exactly what she's doing, he thought. A girl like that knows. She knows what she's doing. It's a game. To her, it's all a game. And she loves it. She loves every minute of it.

After a while, Thomas grew tired of the scotch and of the bar and of the girl and the games. He summoned the waiter and asked for his check. But when he reached across the table to pick it up, he felt the unmistakable touch of a woman on his flesh. Her hand was wrapped tightly around his. He looked up and their eyes met.

"Where are you going?" Kitty asked.

"Home," he replied.

"Buy me a drink before you go?"

"No."

"No?" she asked. "Why not?"

"No," he said.

"That doesn't answer my question," she said.

"It does," he said.

"You've been staring at me all night," she said. "You could at least buy me a drink and make it up to me."

"No," he replied.

"Come on, daddy," she said and she pouted her pouty lips. "I'll make it worth your while."

"Fuck off," he said.

"Hard to get?" she said. "That's ok. I like a challenge."

"Get away from me," he said.

"Don't be an ass," she said. "Look around. Every guy in here wants to take me home. Every guy in here wants to know what it's like. I saw you staring. Don't act like you're any different. The only difference between you and them is that you might actually get to do what they can only dream of."

"I said fuck off," he said. "Now fuck off."

He stuffed a handful of money into the check and got up from the table.

Outside, the snow fell hard and it fell white and it began pile. It covered the sidewalks and the streets and the streetlamps and the cars and the signs and the overhangs. It stuck to the sides of buildings and weighed down the leaves of the palm trees and it fluttered and danced in the wind. And somewhere, in the windowsill of an empty apartment, as if forgotten, there was a pot with fresh cut lilies as clean and as white as the snow that fell and fluttered and danced and stuck to the frozen Pacific earth.

Part 2

Chapter 1

THE SNOWFALL WAS THICK. It made it difficult to see more than a few of feet in front of the truck. It came down fast and heavy in heavy, wet clumps. The wipers struggled to push it from the windshield and it began to pile. He couldn't remember where he was or where he was going and he couldn't remember why. But he knew that he was almost there. He was close. And with every swipe of the blades across the snow covered glass, he was getting closer.

As he drove on, he began to worry that the storm was too severe. What if he never made it? What if he never reached her? He thought of pulling to the side of the highway, turning off the truck, and slowly freezing to death as the snow rose like water up the sides of a sinking ship.

His phone rang and he found the will to live.

"Where are you?" he asked.

"Where I've been," she said.

"I'm on my way," he said. "Wait there."

"I've been waiting," she said. "It's cold. I'm tired."

"I'll be there soon," he said.

"It's cold," she said. "And I'm tired."

"Wait there," he said.

"I might go," she said.

"Wait," he said.

There was no response.

"Wait."

The phone cut out.

"Fuck," he said and slammed his fist into the ceiling. Then he turned on the radio.

"This is a warning from the EMERGENCY BROADCAST SYSTEM," the alert screeched across the speakers. "Thomas, you're driving through intense weather conditions."

"No shit," he said.

"There will be a severe thunderstorm warning in effect until late Sunday night. Settle in by the space heater and prepare for a long evening."

"Thunderstorm?" he snapped. "Are you shitting me?"

"Shut up Thomas," the radio hissed. "Don't be such a prick."

"Anything else?" he said.

"One more thing," the radio replied. "You're a real prick."

"I could've done without that," he said.

"This has been a warning from the EMERGENCY BROAD-CAST SYSTEM. We will now return to our regularly schedule program: *The Wonder Years* radio drama edition starring Fred Savage as the character played by Fred Savage."

"Fuck Fred Savage," Thomas said.

He lit up a cigarette and turned off the radio.

The roads were completely empty. Thomas had gone miles without seeing another car. Of course, he couldn't see much of anything so it was entirely possible that he was surrounded by unseen cars concealed behind the veil of snow. Either way, he was alone. And in the silence, his mind began to wander. He thought of the storm and of the bar and of the waitress and the hotel and the scotch and the games and the girl. He thought of the storm and of the pain and of the ocean and the town and the doctors and the nurses and his wife. He thought of the storm and of the drive and of why and of where and of what he had hoped he would find. Then he thought some more.

It's too cold, she said.

And I'm tired, she said.

And when you get here, I'll already be gone.

A sudden flash ripped Thomas from his thoughts. It was fol-lowed immediately by a piercing crack like a steel train hitting a stone wall. Another flash followed by another crack and he soon realized that a thunderstorm had burst through the belly of the blizzard. With each bolt of lightning, the pounding thunder grew louder and more intense. With each pound of thunder, the lightning crashed and burst and rolled across the sky. The truck shuttered and shook as sky and wind and earth and snow beat down upon it and Thomas choked the wheel.

Flash. Crack. Flash. Crack. The thunder was blinding. The lightning was deafening. The snow was maddening. The truck was sinking. Hail and wind and snow and wind rocked the toy machine back and forth, back and forth, like a child swinging wildly from a rope. Every time he pumped the breaks, his tires slid on the wet road which was now layered with ice and snow and hail and wind. There was no traction. There was no stopping. He was spinning out of control.

Thomas couldn't see past the nose of his truck. Yet he sensed—no, he saw—a figure standing about twenty yards up in the middle of the road. There was a person about twenty yards up in the middle of the road. A woman in the road. She wore a flowing white gown which flapped and flowed and danced in the wind and her eyes were grave and sober. It was cold and she was tired and she shivered and shook as snow and wind and ice and wind broke over her pale flesh.

Thomas lost his reason. Instincts took over as he swerved to avoid his motionless bride. He lost control of the turning vehicle and it gyred down the highway slamming into the median and bouncing back to the street. Anarchy was loosed upon the world as nuts and bolts and glass and terror tore through the air like a scapula through flesh. The truck—or what was left of it—scraped along the guardrail and an explosion of sparks illuminated the frozen Valley sky.

The mangled wreckage soon rolled halt in the right lane of the highway. Thomas forced open the driver's side door and fell to the snow-covered street. Short of breath, he sucked in the icy air. It numbed his lungs. He stumbled to his feet, slipping on the cracked pavement as he rose. Panic filled his mind. Had he hit her? Had he lost her? Was she already gone?

He quickly turned and ran face first into the storm.

"Hey! Hey!" his voice echoed down the unseen stretch of road. "Hey! Are you alright?"

No response.

"Monica?" he screamed into the darkness. "Monica?"

The darkness did not answer.

"Are you ok?" he shouted. "Are you there?"

The wind pounded against his battered flesh.

Flash. Crack. A reverberation of thunder shook the ground beneath his feet. His legs shuddered and he fell to his knees. The snow was falling harder now. It fell hard and it fell white and the wind blew gusts and circles which spun and danced and beat and broke over his broken body. He struggled to open his eyes. When he did, he saw nothing.

"Monica!" he cried out. "Monica!"

The silence was deafening.

"Monica!" he tried. "It's me. I'm here. I made it. I didn't forget you. I didn't forget."

There was no answer.

Thomas awoke from his dream with a start. He found himself lying face down on the grey carpet in his living room. He pulled himself up onto the couch and stretched out. His back ached. He twisted and turned until it cracked. Then he attempted to fall back to sleep. It was no use. He was up.

Chapter 2

KITTY YAWNED, STRETCHED HER arms toward the ceiling, and rolled over without opening her eyes. She wrapped herself tightly around her pillow and decided to sleep off the rest of her hangover. Then she heard the soft shuffle of footsteps and she sprang up in bed.

"Where am I?" she thought as she looked around the dark room. It was not her studio. It was a small bedroom with a queen size bed. The blinds were drawn and no light entered. She could hear someone moving around outside the door. Her head was aching and her stomach tossed and turned. She was wearing an oversized Dodgers t-shirt over her bra and panties. It was not her shirt. Her dress from the night before was laid out on a chair next to the bed. Her mouth tasted like booze and vomit and cinnamon flavored toothpaste. She had a large bruise on her right hip. She had gauze pads tapped to both of her legs. She removed one of the bandages and saw that she had skinned her knee. It was swollen and raw and it hurt to the touch.

When she opened the bedroom door, she found Thomas sitting on the couch. There was a blanket and a pillow on the carpet at his feet. He had a book in one hand and a cigarette in the other.

"Good morning," she said.

He grunted and kept reading.

"Did we . . . ?"

"No," he said. "We didn't."

"Oh," she said. "Why not?"

"I don't have much here," he said. "Do you want some eggs or something?"

At the suggestion her stomach turned.

"Bathroom?" she said with urgency.

He pointed to a door at the end of a long hallway and she hurried over.

When she emerged again, she found him sitting in the same place. He was still reading. He was still smoking.

"You ruined my good shirt last night," he said without looking up.

"Sorry," she said. "I had too much to drink."

He grunted again.

"I'll pay for it," she said.

"I would hope so," he said.

The two sat in an uncomfortable silence.

"Can I ask you something?" she began again.

He let out a long, audible sigh and looked up at her makeup stained face.

"Can I ask you how we ended up here last night?"

"You don't remember?" he said.

She shook her head.

"Figures," he said.

"I'm sorry," she said. "I'll go."

"You won't," he said.

"Excuse me?" she said.

"You won't," he said. "Go."

"Why not?" she asked.

He put down his book.

"I don't know if you were too drunk to notice," he said. "But there was a blizzard last night. There's a blizzard today. No one's going anywhere."

"Right," she said. "I forgot."

"Figures," he said.

"When is it supposed to let up?" she asked.

"Not soon enough," he said.

There was another pause.

"Do you have any water?" she asked.

"Faucet works," he said.

"A glass?" she said.

"Kitchen cabinet," he said. "Where most people keep them."

"Right," she said. "Thanks."

She went to the kitchen and opened the cabinet nearest to the sink.

"Not that one," he called from the other room. "Near the fridge."

"Oh," she said. "Thanks."

She returned to the living room with a glass of water for herself and one for him. She put his on the table in front of him.

"I didn't ask for this," he said.

"Sorry," she said.

Then the two sat in silence. He read and she looked around the room. It was a plain room. No pictures. No artwork. No pots or plants or decorative pillows. There was a TV and a couch and a coffee table and a chair. There were two end tables and a love seat and an ash tray and some coasters. The walls were grey and the windows were grey and the carpet was grey and outside the snow was grey.

Kitty walked to the window.

"I haven't seen snow like this in years," she said.

"Mmm . . ."

"How long is it supposed to last?"

"Too long," he said.

"Did I do something?" she said.

"No," he said.

"You seem upset with me," she said.

"No," he said.

"Then what's bothering you?"

"You being here," he said.

"I'm sorry," she said. "I don't even know how I got here."

He grunted.

"Is there anything I can do?" she said. "To fix it? To make you feel better?"

"No," he said.

"Are you sure?" she said. "There's no way I can make it up to you?"

"No," he said.

"Will you let me try?"

"No," he said.

She slowly strutted from the window to the couch. There, she pulled his oversized t-shirt over her head and stood before him wearing nothing but black lace lingerie.

"I know I've been a bad girl," she said. "How can I make it right?"

He took a long, slow drag on his cigarette. Then he leaned forward and pressed the smoldering butt into the ashtray on the coffee table. The sweet smell of nicotine filled the room.

"Last night," he said.

"Last night," she whispered in her most seductive voice.

"Last night, I held your hair while you puked all over my bathroom. That didn't happen once. It happened several times. One of those times, you missed the toilet and ruined my favorite shirt."

She picked up the oversized Dodger's shirt, pulled it back over her head, slouched down on the loveseat, and covered her face with her hands.

He picked up his book and continued to read.

Chapter 3

HE USED TO TAKE her to dinner on Saturday nights. She'd spend the morning getting her hair done or her nails done or shopping for a new dress—something simple but beautiful. Then she'd go to the church and sit in the very last pew reading Kierkegaard until it was time for confession. She'd enter the confessional, fix herself down on the kneeler, beg the priest for his blessing, and confess her sins. About halfway through, she'd lose herself and begin to tear up. The priest would offer her tissues and forgiveness and she'd accept both. She'd exit back into the church and sit in the very last pew reading poetry—Hardy or Eliot or Browning—until it was time for the four o'clock Vigil Mass. She'd follow the readings in the missal and listen intently to the homily. She'd kneel when she was supposed to kneel and stand when she was supposed to stand and bless herself when it seemed natural to do so. After Mass, she'd drive over to the restaurant. She'd enter wearing her new dress and tell the hostess that she was meeting someone. Then, before she could be directed to the table, she'd spot him sitting with his back to the entrance.

"Never mind," she'd say. "I see him."

She'd walk up behind him and put her hands over his eyes.

"Hmm," he'd say as he rubbed his palms along her arms. "Bill?"

"How'd you guess?" she'd ask and she'd kiss his cheek.

He'd stand and she'd see that he bought her flowers.

"Lilies," she'd say. "My favorite."

"Not from me," he'd say and he'd sip his scotch.

"Uh oh," she'd say as she lifted the bouquet to her nose.

"Should I be worried?" he'd ask.

"No," she'd smile. "*You're* the other man."

"Oh is that so?" he'd laugh.

"It is. But don't worry. My husband's a dope. He'll never figure us out."

"He is a dope," he'd say. "But he's a handsome dope. And don't forget—you're the one who married him."

"Best decision I've ever made," she'd say.

He'd take her hand and he'd kiss it. Then they'd sit.

"So how was your day?" he'd ask. "New dress?"

She'd smile.

"My husband may be a dope," she'd say. "But he doesn't miss a thing."

"I am what I am," he'd say.

Then they'd pick up their menus and search for typos. Whoever found the fewest had to pay for dinner. He always paid—even when he found the most.

One Saturday, the evening was progressing in its usual fashion when suddenly the conversation was cut short.

"I know how this ends," she said plainly.

"A few more glasses of scotch and you on top of me when we get home?"

"Thomas," she said. "Be serious."

"Ok," he said. "Me on top of you."

She looked at him with sober eyes.

"What's the matter?" he said.

"Nothing," she said.

"What is it?" he said. "Something's up."

"It's nothing," she said. "Really."

"Ok," he said.

"It's just . . . " she paused.

"It's just?"

"I was thinking. During Mass. That's all."

"You were thinking? During Mass? That's all?"

"That's all," she said.

"Well what were you thinking?" he said.

"I don't know," she said.

"You don't know what you were thinking?" he said.

"I was thinking about us," she said. "About you and about me."

"Shit," he smiled. "What'd I do this time?"

"Nothing," she said. "It's nothing. Really."

"Come on," he said. "Talk to me."

"Sometimes the priests get cute with their homilies," she said. "Sometimes they tell a story or a joke instead of talking about the readings."

"Sometimes?" he said.

"Once in a while," she said.

"More often than not," he said.

"You would know?" she said.

"Fair point," he said. "Go on."

"Well today was one of the *more often than nots,*" she said.

"What was the joke?" he said.

"No joke," she said. "No story either. A question."

"A question?" he said.

"A question," she said.

"What was the question?" he said.

"What would you ask God if you could ask him anything at all?"

"This is what's got you bent of shape?" he said.

She nodded.

"What would you ask?" he said.

"I would ask why it has to be so hard," she said. "I would ask why he makes things so hard. It doesn't seem right. It doesn't seem fair."

"It's not right," he said. "It's not fair."

There was a long pause. He took a sip of his scotch and let it sit at the back of his throat until it burned the back of his throat. Then he swallowed.

"I know how this ends," she said. "I see our future."

"Tell me," he said. "Will I be rich? Should I avoid leaving the country?"

"No matter how good things are," she said. "No matter how happy we are, it all ends the same. No matter how long this lasts, it won't last. It can't last. Someday it'll be over. Someday it'll all be over. Someday we'll have nothing left. And that crushes me."

He sipped his scotch and let her words settle in.

"I'm sorry," he said.

"For what?" she said.

"For you," he said. "Sorry you still don't see how persistent I am. Sorry you still haven't realized that you're stuck with me."

"Thomas," she said.

"Now I know," he continued. "I know we've had our trials. I know you carry those scars. I wish to hell you didn't have to. I wish I hadn't been such an ass. But I can't change what I've done. I can't take it back and I won't make excuses. All I can do is own it. I'm sorry for what I did. I was an ass. I didn't appreciate you. I hurt you. But I promise that that will never happen again. I promise— I'm not going anywhere."

"Oh Thomas," she said. "You are an ass. You're such an ass. It's not about that. We've worked through that. It's not that. Not this time."

"What then?" he said.

"It's this," she said. "It's these dinners. It's these lilies. It's you and it's me."

"I thought you liked lilies," he said. "I thought you liked you and me."

"I do," she said. "You know I do."

"Then what's the problem?" he said.

She let out a long sigh and looked at the empty table to their right.

"I put that ring on your finger," he said. "You accepted it. It's too late now. You're stuck with me. I'm stuck with you. From this day until our last. Until death do us part."

Again she sighed.

He took her hands in his.

"I'll always be here," he said. "You won't ever have to spend another day without me."

She looked down at the table.

"So then you think that I'm going to die before you?" she said and looked up at him with serious eyes.

Then she burst into laughter.

And so did he.

Chapter 4

"Tell me," said Mary. "Was he as wrinkly as he looked?"

Kitty poured some sugar into her coffee, stirred it slowly, puckered her lips, and blew the steam off the top.

"He must've had a heart attack when you got undressed."

"Be nice," said Kitty. "He was actually kind of sweet."

"Sweet?" said Mary. "He looked like he was about ready to die."

"Would you relax?" said Kitty. "I didn't even sleep with him."

"You didn't?" said Mary.

"No," said Kitty. "He wasn't my type."

"Oh thank God!" Mary exclaimed. "Though I didn't know you had a type."

"Well I do," said Kitty and she dipped her frosted donut down into her mug. "It was, however, a fruitful visit."

"But you didn't sleep with him?"

"Nope."

"Tell me, tell me," said Mary. "I want details. I want a story."

"That's why we're here, isn't it?"

"I'm dying to know," she said. "What did you do all night? Why didn't you sleep with him? What's his house like? Where does he live?"

"What time did I leave the bar?" asked Kitty.

"Probably around midnight," said Mary. "You were pretty wasted."

"I was very wasted," Kitty agreed. "Believe me—I wouldn't have gone home with him if I wasn't."

"I'm surprised you went home with him period," said Mary.

"Me too," said Kitty. "Me too."

"Tell me everything," Mary insisted. "Start from the beginning."

"Ok," said Kitty. "So early on in the night, I was talking to that really cute guy at the bar. You remember him, right?"

Mary nodded.

"Well I was talking to him and whispering in his ear and nibbling on his ear and kissing his neck."

"I remember," said Mary. "It was a bit much."

"Anyway," said Kitty. "I was hanging on his neck and kissing his mouth and that's when his phone started to ring and ring. 'Who is it?' I asked. 'No one,' he said. 'Just a friend.'

"We started hooking up again but his phone kept ringing and ringing and ringing. 'Answer it,' I said. 'Go on.' So he did. Well it turns out that he had a wife at home and two young kids. The youngest one stuck a Lego up his nose—he wanted to see what it smelled like—and his wife couldn't get it out. They were on their way to ER. She wasn't asking him to leave. Apparently he hadn't seen his buddies in a while and she wanted him to have a night out. But she thought that he should know what was going on.

"Now you know me. I'm no moralist. I don't usually give a shit what people do with their personal lives. I've cheated and I've been cheated. I like to think that I've been cheated more than I've cheated but only God knows. I just hope he isn't keeping score."

"You and me both," said Mary.

"Anyway," said Kitty. "When I heard that this guy had a little kid and when I heard that that kid was going to the hospital and when I realized he was planning on going home with me instead of being with his son—well that just didn't sit right. I mean, he was good looking and all. But that's kind of messed up, right?"

"I guess so," said Mary.

"Anyway," Kitty continued. "When he got off the phone and told me what was going on, I told him that I didn't feel so good.

I was trying to be nice. I could've told him he was a douche but I didn't. I just told him that I didn't feel good.

"'You're full of shit,' he said. 'You're just pissed that I have a wife.'

"'You're drunk,' I said. 'Go spend the night with your friends. That's why you're here, isn't it?'

"'I'm not drunk,' he said and he grabbed my arm.

"'Get your hands off me,' I said and I slapped him.

"'You're nothing but a worthless whore,' he said. 'I know you. I know what you do. I know who you are. Whore.' Then he walked away."

"What an ass," Mary said.

Kitty nodded.

"So then what happened?"

"Well that didn't sit well with me. In fact, it really pissed me off. So I decided: no more going home with assholes. Tonight, I just want enjoy being out. Tonight, I want to enjoy being me."

"Good for you," said Mary. "But then how did you end up with that old guy?"

"I looked for you and saw you had a guy of your own. I wasn't going to ruin your good time. That's when I spotted him sitting by himself at one of the tall tables near the bar. I wasn't in the mood to be hit on. I wasn't in the mood to talk to someone whose main interest was getting in my pants. But I was in the mood for a drink and I didn't have any money. So I went over to him and asked him to buy me a drink. He did and we got to talking . . . and flirting."

"You were flirting with that old man?" Mary giggled.

"He was sweet," said Kitty. "His name was Teddy and he showed me pictures of his grandkids. They were cute."

"I'm on the edge of my seat," said Mary.

"Oh stop," said Kitty. "Anyway, he bought me a few drinks. Then a few more. And before I knew it, I was leaving with him. He told me that I was beautiful. He kept saying it: 'you're beautiful.' He said that he had lots of money and that he had no one to spend it on. He used to buy his wife jewelry all the time. But she's dead. He said that he'd buy me jewelry and other nice things because he liked to spend his money but he had no one to spend it on and because I was so beautiful that I ought to have nice things. He even got the door for me when I was getting out of his car."

"Sweet," said Mary.

"It was sweet," Kitty said.

"So what happened next?"

"Nothing happened next."

"Nothing?"

"Not a thing. When we got inside, we went to his bedroom. I asked if I could use his bathroom to freshen up. It was enormous. Two sinks, two mirrors, a shower, a tub, a toilet with a bidet. There were lots of pills near the sink but I didn't see what they were. I didn't want to know. I just washed up, put some fresh makeup on my face, slipped out of my dress, and when I went back into the bedroom . . . "

"When you went back into the bedroom?"

"When I went back . . . he was asleep."

Mary burst into laughter.

"Oh stop it," said Kitty. "I can't tell you anything."

"I'm sorry," Mary cried. "I'm sorry. But that's great. He was asleep!"

"Quiet you," said Kitty.

"I'm sorry," she said and she took a deep breath. "I'm sorry. I just can't help but to imagine you standing there in front of his bathroom mirror trying to mentally prepare yourself to sleep with that wrinkly, old bag . . . "

"Teddy," she said. "His name was Teddy."

"Teddy," said Mary. "Trying to mentally prepare yourself to sleep with Teddy, and when you come out wearing nothing but a pair of lace panties, there he is—dead asleep."

"It is kind of funny," said Kitty.

"Was he snoring?" asked Mary.

"Oh, brutally," said Kitty.

The two laughed.

"You poor girl," said Mary. "You poor, poor girl. You spend your entire night with that old man and he does what old men do. He falls asleep before the best part. What a travesty."

"Well," said Kitty. "It wasn't a total loss."

"What do you mean?" asked Mary.

Kitty pulled back her hair and revealed a pair of pearl earrings.

"Pretty," said Mary. "He gave those to you?"

"You could say that," she said.

"Oh, you didn't!" Mary cried out.

"Well, they were just sitting on his dresser collecting dust."

"You stole an old man's pearl earrings?" laughed Mary. "They probably belonged to his dead wife!"

"I didn't steal anything," said Kitty. "He promised to buy me jewelry. His wife's dead and he has no one to spend his money on. I'm beautiful and I deserve to have nice things. He said it. Not me. It's not my fault that he fell asleep before he had a chance to live up to his word."

"So you went shopping without him," she said.

"Exactly," said Kitty. "He would have given them to me anyway. It's almost as if he did."

"But he didn't," laughed Mary.

"Who's the moralist now?" said Kitty.

"Believe me," said Mary. "I'm no moralist. I just think we should call a spade a spade and admit that you stole them. After all, you did steal them."

"Then I stole them," said Kitty. "Honestly, what does it matter?"

"Wait," said Mary. "I have an idea."

"What do you mean you have an idea?"

"Call it a challenge. No, no—a game. Like a scavenger hunt!"

"What are you talking about?" said Kitty.

"It's perfect," said Mary. "It's too perfect."

"What is?" said Kitty. "Tell me."

"What if, instead of coming to this diner to trade stories about the assholes we slept with, we come to trade treasures from the assholes we slept with?"

"I don't follow," said Kitty.

"What if we make a game of it?" said Mary. "These guys take us home and treat us like whores. Some of them even call us whores. It's not right. It's not fair."

"Ok," said Kitty. "But what are you suggesting we do?"

"I'm suggesting we get even," said Mary. "I'm suggesting we have a little fun. These guys go out to clubs and they prey on women like us. And for the most part, we're fine with being their prey. But what if we stop being the hunted and start being the hunters?"

"Are you saying . . . "

"Yes," said Mary. "That's exactly what I'm saying."

"That's so mean," said Kitty. "That's really a nasty idea. And I love it."

Chapter 5

AFTER LEAVING THE HOTEL bar in huff, Thomas had sat in the
parking garage for a full twenty minutes. He smoked a cigarette
and drank a bottle of water. He wanted to make sure that he was
sober enough to drive home in the snow. When he pulled out of
the garage, the snowfall was thick. It was difficult to see more than
a few of feet in front of his truck. It came down fast and heavy in
heavy, wet clumps. The wipers struggled to push it from the windshield and it began to pile. As he drove past the hotel, he slowed
the truck and scanned the building from the outside. He took a
long drag on his cigarette and drove on.

About a block up the road, he rolled to a stop at a traffic light.
Steam rose like smoke from his hood as the wet flakes melted on
the hot engine. It was coming down hard now. He could barely see.
But as his eyes peered through the frost covered windshield, he
noticed something on the sidewalk. He leaned over and used the
sleeve of his favorite shirt to rub the fog from his passenger's side
window. His eyes were not deceiving him. There lying motionless
on the pavement was a large black clump half covered with snow.

Damn Mexicans, he thought. They can't just bring their shit
to the dump like everyone else. They've got to liter our streets with
their trash.

As he waited for the light to change, he continued to stare. He
wiped the fog from his window once more and rubbed his eyes.
They must be playing tricks, he thought. It looked like that bag of

trash was rolling around on the cement. Was it a bag of trash? Was it something else? What else could it be?

He rubbed his eyes again and stared intently at the mysterious mound. But the sudden blast of car horn ripped him from his thoughts. The light had changed and he was holding up traffic. He drove on for a few blocks and resolved to just head home. He'd had too much to drink. He was probably seeing things. It was just a bag of trash or a heap of newspapers or some ratty old sweater. But what if it wasn't? What if it was something else? What if it was *someone* else? What if it was a person?

Well—so what if it was? That wasn't any of his business. He wasn't responsible for the things that other people did. He wasn't responsible for the situations they found themselves in. That's what the police were for. That's why he paid his taxes. It wasn't his job. He couldn't save anyone. He couldn't fix anything. Besides, he was too drunk to be driving all over town. What was he supposed to do—turn the truck around and run the risk of getting arrested? All for a lousy bag of trash?

"Fuck," he said and he turned the truck around.

When he pulled up, he knew his intuition had been right. It was a person. He could feel it. He parked on the side of the road, put on his hazards, and stepped out into the snow.

"Hey!" he called over. "Hey! Are you alright?"

No response.

He waited for a car to pass and then ran across the snow covered street. When he reached the other side, he saw her—frail and broken, shivering and shaking on the cold cement.

"I don't want to get up," she cried. "Leave me here."

He bent down and put his jacket over her.

"You're hurt," he said.

"Leave me," she said. "I want to die."

"Should I call for help?" he said.

"Leave me!" she shouted.

"No," he said.

"It's cold," she said. "It's so cold."

"I know," he said. "You're shaking."

"It's cold," she said.

"Can you stand?" he said.

"I'm drunk," she said. "I'm sorry, I'm drunk. I'm so drunk."

"It's ok," he said. "You're bleeding."

"My heel broke," she said. "My heel broke and I'm drunk."

"You're bleeding," he said.

"I skinned my knees," she said. "I skinned my knees and I'm drunk."

"It's ok," he said. "I'll take you home. Where do you live?"

"Not there," she said. "I hate it. I can't go. Not tonight. Not there. Anywhere but there. I'm so drunk."

"Can you stand?" he asked.

"I don't want to," she said.

"Don't make me carry you," he said. "I'll carry you if I have to."

"Lift me," she said.

"Are you sure?" he said.

"Lift me," she said.

Thomas put his arms on the frozen ground and cradled her like an infant. As he stood, a sharp pain shot down his spine. He cringed.

"You're strong," she whispered. "You're so strong."

Then she nestled her face into his shoulder.

He looked down at the girl bundled up in his arms. She was so young. She was so hurt. She was so broken. He looked at her torn dress and her snow covered hair. He looked at her skinned knees and her frostbitten lips. He looked at her sweet face and her soft dimples and her sincere eyes. She looked like an angel. A fallen angel. A broken angel.

"Where are you taking me?" she said.

"Where do you live?" he said.

"No," she said. "Not there. Please."

"Then where?" he asked.

"Home," she said. "I want to go home."

He carried her across the street and lifted her up into the truck. Then he buckled her seatbelt and she fell asleep.

Chapter 6

THE HOSPITAL WAS COLD and it was clean and it was sterile. It smelled like rubbing alcohol and latex and soiled linens and bleach. The incessant shuffle of doctors and nurses and janitors coming and going from one room to the next was drowned out by the incessant beeping of heart rate monitors and the incessant dripping of IV drips.

"Where do I have to go to make a phone call?" a man asked one of the nurses.

He pointed to a sign which read *Please No Cell Phones: They Interfere With Our Telemetry Units.*

"Oh that's ok," she said. "You're fine."

Thomas sat in a nearby office wondering why airlines and hospitals insisted upon lying to the general public. Are people so unreasonable that a simple *"Please no cell phones because no one is interested in spending a six hour flight next to the woman who 'just can't believe what her coworker said behind her back'"* wouldn't suffice?

"What are you thinking?" she said.

"I hate hospitals," he said.

"Who likes them?" she said.

"No one, I suppose. But I hate them. I really do. Can you think of any place you'd rather be less than this hospital? It's cold and dry and filled with artificial light. It's too hygienic. It's too clean. It makes me want to go out and roll in the mud."

"I'd pay to see that," she smiled. "But as far as hospitals go, this one isn't that bad."

"As far as hospitals go," he said. "That's the important part. I don't hate this specific hospital. I hate all hospitals. I hate the Platonic Form of hospitals. They're all the same. They're all terrible. And it's not for lack of trying. Every one of them—every goddamned one—has pots with fresh green plants and framed prints of famous frescos. Usually something flowery. A Monet. A girl sitting by a lake in the typical Monet style. And every one of them—every last one—is the most morbid, sterile, suffocating place on earth. I don't know what it is. It has something to do with the tight corridors or the tile floors or the hand sanitizers or the white walls."

"Or the people dying," she added.

He paused.

"Oh come on," she said. "That was supposed to be funny."

"I know," he said. "I know it was. Anyway, I'm only ranting. I rant when I'm nervous."

"I love your rants," she said. "That's why I married you."

"I'm done," he said. "I'm done now."

"Don't be that way," she said. "I was only kidding. Besides, I like your rants. They make me feel better. They make me feel sane. Go on. Make me feel sane."

"I lost it," he said.

"Please," she said and she took his hand in hers. "I'm cold and I'm tired and I just want to hear one of your rants."

"Well I was thinking," he said.

"Yes. Tell me, darling."

"I was thinking of how maddening it is when people rail against the Catholics for storing up all that artwork—all those priceless sculptures and statues and paintings and books. You know people actually say they should sell all of it and give the money to charity? Aren't people who talk like that lunatics? Don't those people strike you as mentally unstable?"

"Depends on whose diagnosing, I suppose."

"Honestly," he continued. "I'm no supporter of the Pope. You know that. But people who speak of it in that way—as if robbing the world of its beauty will solve the injustice. As if people who suffer need bread more than they need life. It's so utilitarian. It's so sterile. People who spew that garbage haven't spent much time in hospitals. I can assure you that. If they had, they'd know. Beauty saves."

There was a knock at the door and in came the doctor.

"So now that you have the results," he said. "Let's talk about where we go from here."

Chapter 7

"WILL IT HURT?" SHE asked.

"You'll feel some slight discomfort," he said. "Most girls are fully recovered and back to normal activity in about two months time."

"And then I can go back to work?"

"We recommend that our patients wait at least six weeks before engaging in any type of serious physical activity," he said.

She laughed. Then, seeing that wasn't trying to be funny, she blushed.

"But honestly," he continued. "It depends on how you're feeling."

"I'm sorry about all the questions," she said and she looked down at the tile floor.

"Don't be," he said. "It's our job to make sure that you're completely aware of how this procedure will work. It's our job to make you feel as comfortable as possible. Now if you'll just slide your butt forward and spread your knees for me, I need to take a look."

As she repositioned herself on the cold, hard table, her bare thighs stuck to the cold, hard steel.

"Will he feel anything?" she said.

"No, no," he said with a reassuring smile. "We take every precaution to make sure that it doesn't feel a thing. Before you leave here today, we'll give you some pills. You'll take one dose here in the office and another a few days from now at home. That should bring it off. By the time you come back for your next appointment, it'll be done with. It'll all be over. No mess. No fuss. It's really an awfully simple procedure. It's perfectly simple."

"And it'll be gone? Nothing to fix?"

"When you come in, we'll remove anything that hasn't made its way out already."

"Does it come out . . . in parts?"

He smiled.

"No, no," he said. "You're relatively early on. You can expect a lot of bleeding. There shouldn't be much more than that."

"Is that natural?" she said.

"It's normal, yes."

"Oh," she said. "And it's completely safe?"

"Kitty," he said and he looked into her eyes. "I assure you that this procedure is very common. It's very simple. Every day you walk past dozens of women who have had to deal with similar issues."

"That's true," she said.

"Think of it like this," he said. "I have a friend who's a derma-tologist. In a year's time, he removes about two hundred moles to biopsy for cancer. We perform the same number of these proce-dures here every few months. You wouldn't be overly concerned about having a mole biopsied, would you?"

"If I thought I had cancer," she said.

He laughed.

"I mean the procedure itself," he said.

"Oh," she blushed. "I guess not."

"Exactly," he said. "So you see—there's nothing to worry about."

"I know doctor. I know you're right. It's just a bit overwhelm-ing, you know?"

"It's ok," he said. "It's ok to be nervous. But I promise you, everything will be alright. You're actually pretty lucky."

"Lucky?" she said.

"Lucky," he said. "You caught it early, thank God. You wouldn't believe how many women come through that door when it's almost too late. We try our best to take care of them, of course.

We do what we can. But it's a lot more difficult. It's a lot more paperwork too."

She smiled.

He put his hand on her knee.

"You'll be alright. I promise. In two months time, everything will go back to normal. This whole nightmare will be behind you. That's what we do here. We fix problems."

He finished the exam, threw his latex gloves in the trash, and lathered his hands with soap and sanitizer.

"You're shaking," he said.

"It's cold," she said. "The table."

"The steel," he said.

She nodded.

"Easier to clean," he said. "It's very important that we have a sterile environment. We care about our patients here. We want them to be safe."

She nodded again.

"Well," he said. "If you have no further questions, I'll go get that medication and we'll get this ugliness over with."

"Ugliness?" she said.

The word sounded as strange coming from her mouth as it had from his.

"Unpleasantness," he said. "It's an expression."

"An expression," she said.

He walked out of the room.

When he returned, he found her out of her gown and fully clothed. She was shaking.

"What's wrong?" he said.

"I'm sorry doctor," she said. "I'm sorry."

"You're shaking," he said.

"I'm sorry," she said.

"I understand," he said. "But I have to remind you that the sooner you do it, the simpler it'll be."

"I'm sorry," she said.

"There now," he said and he put his hand on her shoulder. "There now, it's ok. It's a big decision. I get that. Take all the time you need to think it over. We'll be waiting here when you get back."

"Thank you," she said.

As she walked down the long, white hallway with its white walls and its white tiles and its white lighting, she paused and thought of going back. At the end of the hall was a red Exit sign. Its red letters flickered on and off, on and off. She stared at it. Then, taking a deep breath, she made her way to the door. She pushed it open with both hands and stepped out into the light. It was a bright April morning. She squinted and rubbed her eyes until they adjusted to the sun. Its warm rays warmed her cheeks and she directed her face up toward the sky. Then her phone rang.

"Hello?" she said.

"How'd it go?" he asked.

"I took care of it," she said. "You're off the hook."

"Oh thank God," he said.

"Goodbye," she said and hung up.

When she got in her car, she rolled down the windows, buckled her seatbelt, and started the engine. Then, without thinking, she picked up her phone, and dialed. It rang once. She hung up immediately and flung the phone on the seat next to her.

"Shit, shit, shit, shit."

It began to vibrate.

"Hello?" her voice cracked.

"Sis?"

She didn't answer.

"Sis? You there?"

"Hey," she said.

"Hey," he said. "I think you called but when I picked up it cut out."

"Sorry," she said.

"Is everything ok?" he said.

"I didn't go through with it," she said. "I decided not to go through with it. I just thought you should know."

"Oh thank God," he said. "We've been praying for you."

She hung up and when her phone rang again, she ignored it.

Chapter 8

"Any treasures?" the text read.

"None yet," she texted back. "Where are you?"

"Stuck at some guy's place," texted Mary. "Plenty of good stuff here. Just gotta sneak something out. You?"

"Stuck at some guy's place," texted Kitty. "Did you see me leave last night?"

"Nope. We left before you."

"Ok. Be safe," Kitty texted. "Love ya."

"Love ya girly," texted Mary. "Don't forget to find something good!"

Kitty put her phone in her handbag and looked over at Thomas. He was still reading. The two hadn't spoken in over an hour. She felt tense and uneasy and the fact that he seemed so comfortable with the silence made her resent him. She got up and walked to the window. Much to her chagrin, the snow seemed to be coming down as heavily as before. She was trapped.

"Can I take a shower?" she said.

"Shower's busted," he said without looking up.

"How do you get clean?" she said.

"Tub works," he said.

"Can I take a bath?" she said.

"No one's stopping you," he said.

"You know, you're not much of a host," she said.

"I am what I am," he said.

"Right," she said and she glared at him.

He didn't notice.

"Where can I find a towel?" she said.

"There's a closet in the bedroom," he said.

"Thanks," she said.

He grunted.

She walked down the hall and left him sitting there. When she entered the room in which she had slept, she turned on the lamp, and looked around. It was a small bedroom with a queen size bed. The blinds were drawn and no light entered. It was plain and it was modest and it was boring. She walked to the closet and found the towels stacked neatly on the top shelf. She pulled one down and began to undress. As she slid her black panties to her ankles, she felt them rub against her raw skin, and she winced in pain. The cuts were sore and raw and they were swollen and deep. Her flesh was scabbed and bruised and raw and tender. It hurt to the touch.

On the wall opposite the door was a bureau with a mirror. She stood before the fingerprint smudged glass and examined the reflection of her body. She started by probing at the cuts on her legs. But as she continued to stare, she soon found herself scrutinizing herself from head to toe.

"What a mess," she said and she pulled on her face. Her makeup was smudged and smeared and her hair frizzed and fluffed in all the wrong places. She ran her fingers through it and they got stuck. Then she looked at her shoulders and at her belly and at her thighs and her back. She looked at her legs and at her hips and at her butt. Then at her neck. Then at her breasts. One studio had offered to pay for her to have them done. She was glad that she'd decided not to. She liked her breasts. They weren't big but they were real. They were hers.

She wrapped her towel around her and sat on the edge of the bed. There was a small nightstand at her side. She pulled open the top drawer. It was full of letters and notes and pictures of Thomas with his arm around a woman's shoulder. Beneath the clutter were an old, leather bound Bible and a worn, wooden rosary which looked as if it hadn't been used in years. *Don't forget to find something good*, she thought. She held the rosary in the palm of her hand and wrapped its beads around her fingers. She rubbed her thumb over its wooden god and gazed down at his sunken face. Then she let out a hollow sigh.

"Just do it already," she said and she stuffed it into her handbag, crucifix first. She closed the draw and got up to leave. But when she reached the door, she noticed that she had left the Bible sitting on the bed. She walked over and, without knowing why, began thumbing through. The pages of the old book were yellow and moldy and they stuck together. It opened on a page with a Mass card stuffed inside. On the front of the card was an image of a woman drying Christ's feet with her hair. On the back, the words *In Loving Memory of Monica Fontane* were printed in black ink above a prayer to the Sacred Heart of Jesus. Kitty placed the card on the bed next to her and began to read from the Bible.

"When the Jews who were in the house comforting Mary saw her get up so quickly and go out, they followed her, thinking that she was going to the tomb to weep there. Mary went to Jesus, and as soon as she saw him she threw herself at his feet, saying, 'Lord, if you had been here, my brother would not have died.' At the sight of her tears, and those of the Jews who had come with her, Jesus was greatly distressed, and with a profound sigh he said, 'Where have you put him?' They said, 'Lord, come and see.' Jesus wept."

"What the fuck do you think you're doing?" he said.

Kitty turned and saw Thomas standing in the doorway.

"Who the fuck do you think you are?"

"I'm sorry," she said. "I didn't . . . I don't . . . "

"Get out of my room."

"I'm sorry," she said. "I'm sorry."

"Get out!" he yelled and he banged his fist against the wall.

She stuffed the Bible back in the drawer and closed it. Then she pushed past Thomas with one hand holding up her towel and the other covering her face. She ran into the bathroom, slammed the door shut, and laid down on the tile floor.

Kitty wept.

Chapter 9

"ARE YOU ASLEEP?" SHE said from the couch.

"I can't sleep," he said.

"Well of course not," she said. "Your back must be killing you."

"No," he said. "It's not that."

"Of course it's that," she said. "The floor's no place for a grown man to sleep."

"It's not my back," he said. "It's not the floor. I'm perfectly comfortable."

"You can't be comfortable," she said. "Not on the floor."

"It's not the floor," he said. "It's not that."

"Then what?" she said.

"It's you," he said.

"I'm sorry," she said.

"Don't be," he said. "It's not your fault."

There was a long pause.

"I wish you'd go to the bedroom," she said.

"Will you go with me?" he said.

"You know I can't sleep there," she said. "You know it's not comfortable for me. I bleed and stick to the sheets."

"I know," he said. "I know."

"I wish you'd go get some rest," she said.

"If you're out here, I'm out here," he said.

"But I have to be out here," she said.

"So do I," he said. "Stop asking me to leave."

"It's not fair to you," she said. "It's not right."

"I'm here and I'm staying," he said.

"Will you at least sleep on the loveseat?" she said.

"I want to be next to you," he said. "The floor's fine."

"Then why can't you sleep?" she said.

"Because I can't," he said.

"Why not?" she said.

"Because I'm scared," he said.

"Me too," she said. "I'm scared too."

The next morning, he wouldn't touch his breakfast.

"Aren't you going to eat?" she said. "It's getting cold."

"I can't eat," he said. "I have no appetite."

"Don't be that way," she said. "You can't just let yourself starve."

"Can't I?" he said.

"No," she said. "I need you healthy. I need you at full strength."

"I have no strength," he said.

"Come on," she said. "Don't be like that."

"How should I be?" he asked.

"I'm the one who's sick," she said. "Not you, remember? If anyone should be down it should be me."

"I wish it was me," he said.

"No you don't," she said.

"I do," he said. "I'd give anything for it to be me."

"Well I wouldn't," she said. "I need you at full strength. That way you can take care of me."

"Who's going to take care of me?" he said.

"Remember when we moved here?" she said. "Remember the drive?"

"I remember," he said.

"It was so hot," she said. "It was such a long drive."

"It was," he said.

"The middle of summer," she said. "Who would be dumb enough to drive halfway across the country in the middle of summer?"

"We would," he said.

"We did," she said. "That heat wave was brutal."

"It was," he said.

"Remember how I got car sick about seven hours in?" she said.

"I remember," he said.

"Remember how you stopped at that rest stop and there was that old man there and he kept eyeballing me?" she said.

"I remember," he said.

"You yelled at him," she said. "That poor old man."

"I didn't like how he was looking at you," he said. "You were sick."

"That poor old man," she said.

"That poor old man," he said.

"Remember how the wind blew my hair in my face?" she said.

"I remember," he said.

"You held it for me," she said. "You held it while I was sick."

"I did," he said.

"Did I ever thank you?" she said.

"I don't remember," he said. "I'm sure you did."

"Well thank you," she said. "That was nice of you."

"It was what it was," he said.

"You didn't want to move," she said.

"I didn't," he said.

"But you moved," she said.

"I did," he said.

"For me," she said.

"For you," he said.

"Was it worth it?" she said.

He looked at her with sober eyes.

"It was," he said.

"Even now?" she said.

"Of course," he said. "I wouldn't change a thing."

There was a long pause and the two looked down at their plates.

"We just have to bear it," she said.

"How do you mean?" he said.

"We just have to bear it," she said. "You heard the doctor. Let's not lie to ourselves. Let's not lie to one another. I'm not going to get well. We can't pretend."

"I know," he said.

"We just have to bear it," she said. "We have to cling to it. We have to love it."

"How?" he said.

"I don't know," she said. "I don't know. But I know we have to. It's too late. We've come too far. It's too late to do anything else. And we have further to go. But there's no going back. Not now. There's no *what could have been*. We're given what we're given. We don't have a say. We don't have a choice. We're given what we're given and the only choice we have is whether we're going to lie to ourselves or we're going to bear it."

"I'm too weak," he said.

"We both are," she said. "But we have to do it anyway. We have to cling to it. We have to love it. We have to wake up each day and ask for it to be harder. We have to want it to be worse. That's the only way. That's the only way."

"I don't want it to get worse," he said. "Not for you."

"I do," she said. "There's no peace in this life."

"It's not fair," he said. "It's not right."

"Bear it," she said. "Bare it with me."

She took his hand in hers and pressed it to her face. Her tears ran over his knuckles.

Then he leaned in and kissed her forehead.

"I'll try," he said. "I'll try."

Chapter 10

ON THE NIGHT HIS sister called, he was drunk. It had been three months since he'd touched the stuff and he had no intention of starting up again. But his wife was out of town and his kids were sleeping over the in-laws' and he had the house to himself and there was nothing to do.

The evening had started off innocently enough. He didn't feel like cooking so he went to a local pizza place to grab a grinder for dinner. While he was waiting for them to make it, an old friend walked through the door. They got to talking and to laughing and to telling stories. Then his friend suggested that they grab a beer and catch up.

"One beer," he said. "Then I have to head out."

"One beer," his friend agreed.

But after the first, he didn't head out. And after the second, he didn't head out. And after the third, he didn't head out. And after the fourth, he stopped counting. The conversation was good and the beer was cold and they talked about sports and politics and religion. The bar was nice and there was nothing else to do and they talked about work and wives and children. They laughed and remembered the good times. They laughed and remembered the bad times. They laughed and drank pitcher after pitcher after pitcher.

"How's your sister been?" asked his friend with genuine concern.

"Actually," he said. "Surprisingly good. She's having a baby."

"No shit?" he said.

"Yeah," he said. "I think it's a really good thing for her. I think it's a real blessing. She quit the business and now she's waitressing at a little diner out there. I'm trying to convince her to move back this way—see if I can get her a job at the bank, you know? Plus we'll help with the baby. Kelly and I invited her out for Thanksgiving. We want to show her what it's like to be around family."

"To Uncle Charlie," said his friend and he raised his glass.

"To Uncle Charlie," he said and he drank it down.

When he got home, he was drunk. He went to the fridge and pulled out the pound of oven roasted turkey breast that his wife had bought for him to make sandwiches while she was away. He sat at the kitchen table and ate it in the darkness—he hadn't turned on the lights. After the fifth or six slice, he noticed that the message light on his answering machine was flashing on and off, on and off. He stuffed another piece of turkey in his mouth and got up to listen.

"Where are you?" cried the voice of his sister through the machine. She sounded frightened. "Where the fuck are you? I don't know what's going on." She was crying. "I keep calling and calling but you're not there. Where are you? I need you."

His heart began to race.

"Charlie?" she cried. "Charlie? I just woke up. I felt something and woke up. And my bed . . . my bed . . . I don't know what's going on. Where are you? I need you. I need you, Charlie. I don't know what's going on. I was asleep and I felt something. It woke me. I woke up. I woke up. And my sheets. My sheets. I need you. I don't know what to do. I don't know who to call. I'm scared. I'm so scared, Charlie."

The machine beeped. The message had ended. And when Charlie called her, she did not answer.

Chapter 11

HER PHONE RANG AND rang. He looked over at her handbag which sat next to him on the bed and wondered who was calling. He wondered if anyone knew where she was. He wondered if anyone cared. He hoped that someone cared. He feared that she was like him. Alone. He feared that she was like him and he regretted having yelled at her. It was an overreaction. He was just tired from the night before. He was just tired of the way things were. He was just tired.

"There's no excuse," he said to himself. "All you can do is own it."

He reached down into her purse, grabbed her phone, and got up to apologize. But when he looked at his hand, he saw that he'd pulled more than her phone from the bag, and he sat back on the bed.

In the bathroom, she filled the tub and slowly lowered her frail body down into the warm bath. It steamed and bubbled and beaded on her naked flesh. She let out a gentle sigh, pressed her eyelids shut, and laid her head back against the plaster rim of the plaster bowl.

Then came a knock upon the door.

"Come in," she said.

The door swung slowly open and he stood in the doorway.

"Listen," she said from the tub. "I want to say that I'm sorry for going through your personal shit."

He stood motionless.

"I know that you welcomed me into your home," she continued. "It wasn't right of me to do that."

He remained silent.

"It was just curiosity," she said. "Girls can be stupid. I was just curious, that's all. I'm sorry."

He stared at her blankly.

"Can you say something?" she said. "Do you forgive me?"

He did not respond.

"It's ok if you don't," she said. "I understand. But can you at least say something?"

He said nothing.

"I'll leave as soon as the storm ends," she said. "You'll never have to see me again."

There was a long silence which lingered and hung in the air. The steam from the tub rose like incense from a censer. It gathered and hung along the ceiling where it condensed into beads which dripped and dropped and ran down the walls. The air was moist and heavy and the windows were covered with fog and steam and moisture and sweat. All was still.

"Say something!" Kitty shouted and she splashed the water with her fists.

"What's your name?" he said.

"Kitty," she said. "Kitty St. Clare."

"No," he said. "Tell me your name."

"I told you," she said. "I'm Kitty St. Clare."

"Your name," he demanded with a dreadful seriousness.

She cupped her breasts with her hands and sank her body beneath the water.

"My name," she said. "Is Kitty . . . "

"No," he interrupted. "Tell me your name."

"My name . . . " she said.

"Your name!" he shouted.

She pulled back as if he was going to rush at her but he remained in the doorway.

"My name," she trembled.

The steam continued to gather at the ceiling.

"Is Lola."

"Lola what?" he said.

"Lola Rosario," she said.

"Lola Rosario," he said.

"Lola Rosario," she said.

"Lola," he said and he held out his hand. "This was my wife's."
Her heart sank.

From his fingers dangled a worn, wooden rosary which looked as if it hadn't been used in years.

"Why?" he said.

"Listen," she said. "I didn't . . . "

He looked down at his hand and began to tremble.

"I'm sorry," she blurted out. "I don't know what I was thinking."

"Why?" he said and he looked up into her eyes. "Why?"

"I don't . . . " she stuttered. "I didn't . . . "

"Why would you take this from me?" he said. "My wife's. It was my wife's."

"I don't know," she cried out. "I don't know! I don't know why I did it."

"My wife's," he repeated. "Her rosary."

"I did it to be mean," she said. "I did it to be nasty. Because I could."

"But why?" he asked. "My wife's rosary."

"I don't know," she cried. "I don't know why I did it. I don't know why I do these things. Because I can. Because I'm ugly. Because I'm fucked up. I'm a mess. A fucking mess. Can't you see? Don't you see? Look at me! I'm a fucking mess."

She pulled on her face and she cried and cried.

"I'm not a bad person," she said. "At least I didn't use to be."

He stood in the doorway and watched. Then he put the wooden beads in his pocket, crucifix first, and entered the room.

"Stupid girl," he whispered.

"I wish you'd just left me," she said. "Last night. I remember. I remember now. I know how I got here. I remember how you came back for me. I remember where you found me. I wish you hadn't. I wish you'd just left me. I wish you'd just let me freeze. I'm so sick of everything. I'm so fucking sick. I wish I was dead. I feel dead. I wish I was."

She was shaking now. She pulled her knees to her chest and rocked herself back and forth, back and forth. She shook and shook and cried and cried. And then she cried some more.

The water poured from the sides of the tub and it puddled on the tile below.

"Stupid girl," he whispered.

"Why didn't you leave me?" she cried. "Why couldn't you have just left me?"

He stepped closer.

"We'd both be better off," she continued. "We'd both be happy. If I wasn't here. If I was dead. We'd both be happy."

He walked slowly to the tub and put his hand on her shoulder.

She pulled away and hid her face in her arms.

"Stupid girl," he said.

Then he bent over and reached down into the water. He didn't roll his sleeves. He just reached in. When he pulled his arms from the tub, his shirt was wet up to the elbows. He had a bar of soap in his hands and he began to lather his hands with the soap.

He touched her shoulder again.

Again she pulled away.

"Stupid girl," he said.

Then he cupped his hands and filled them with water. He poured the water over her back and it glistened and sparkled and glowed. It formed beads on her flesh which he wiped with his hands and he rubbed the bar of soap along her smooth skin. The soap slid and slipped and his palms glided over her wet body. He lifted her arms and washed under her armpits. He washed her shoulders and her neck. He washed her back and her legs. He washed the makeup off of her face and he gently rubbed the scabs on her knees. He washed her breasts and under her breasts and her belly and her thighs. Then, when he reached her feet, he pulled them from the tub, and washed them one at a time. He carefully scrubbed each foot. He was firm but tender with his touch. He lathered them and rinsed them and lathered them and kissed them. Then he emptied the bath and dried her with a towel.

All the while she sat and cried and cried and cried.

"Stupid girl," he said as he toweled her off. "Stupid girl."

He put his arms on the plaster bottom of the plaster tub and cradled her like an infant. As he stood, a sharp pain shot down his spine. He cringed.

"You're strong," she whispered. "You're so strong."

Then she nestled her face into his shoulder.

He looked down at the naked girl bundled up in his arms. She was so young. She was so hurt. She was so broken.

"Stupid girl," he said as he rocked her back and forth. "Stupid girl."

And together they wept.

Chapter 12

SOMEDAY, YEARS FROM NOW, when Lola is old and wrinkled and she has a woman to cook for her and clean for her and bath her and towel her off and when she's dealt with the suffering and the anguish and the sins and the scabs and the scars and when she's coped with the memories of her childhood and the loss of her mother and the baby she bled out and the brother she tore down and the men she cheated and the men who cheated her and the friends she abandoned and when she's cried and cried and cried over the pain and the suffering and the guilt and the stain and when she has no tears left to cry because she's cried them all out and because she's found her peace—on that day, there will be snow in the Valley.

"I haven't seen snow like this in years," the woman who cares for her will say. "Not since before I moved to the Valley."

Then she'll roll Lola's chair to the window and open the blinds and the snow will fall white and it will fall hard and the wind will blow gusts and circles which spin and dance and the snow will fall white and hard.

"I'll bet you've never seen snow like this before," the woman will say.

"Stupid girl," Lola will whisper.

"What's that?" the woman will say.

But Lola won't answer. She'll simply smile and watch as the snowflakes dance down, perfect and white, like whitest of lilies and she'll think of Thomas and of the weekend they spent in his humble apartment and she'll know that he hasn't been forgotten and that neither has she.